Meet the CHARACTERS

Chapter One

Run Run Run

“I... will... beat... you...” Riya panted. Her was face sweaty and her legs ached, but she couldn’t let Emma beat her. It was a sunny afternoon at Greenlake Primary School, and sports day was in full swing. Riya, Emma, and the rest of their class were doing cross country. They had to run around the field not once, not twice, but THREE times.

"I... will... never... lose to you!" Emma gasped. The rest of the class had zoomed ahead. Riya and Emma were left at the back, fighting it out to not come last.

"You won't beat me!" Riya closed her eyes tight and ran with all her might.

She thought that she had pushed ahead but Emma was still next to her. “Go away!”

“Just give up!” Emma yelled.

"No! No! No!" Riya yelled back.

Mr Meridell watched the two girls from the other end of the field and shook his head. He could see that they were arguing, yet again. They were always competing in the classroom and it was the same on the sports field.

"When will those girls

learn to get on?" wondered Mr Meridell. He had been their teacher for a long time. They used to be good friends; they loved sharing books and helping each other out. They used to love sports days too, and when they partnered up for relay races and wheelbarrow races, they would win every time.

Maybe they just needed a little reminder...

Riya huffed and Emma puffed, and they ran and ran, when suddenly... **WHOOSH!** The grass below their feet

disappeared and they started falling. 'Not again!' Riya thought. She looked over at Emma as they fell. Emma was screaming with her eyes closed. Riya reached out and grabbed Emma's arm so she wouldn't fly away. At least Riya wouldn't be alone this time.

Chapter Two

Wonky Wheelbarrows

They landed with a thud. Riya was still holding Emma's arm and Emma pulled it free.

"W-what happened?" Emma said, as she looked around. "Where are we? Where's my PE kit?" Riya looked down. They were both wearing odd dresses. She couldn't tell what hers was made out of, but it felt rough.

“It’s so hot,” Emma said. There was not a single cloud in the sky and the Sun was glaring down at them. “What happened to the school field? Why is the grass so strange?” Emma had so many questions. Riya was about to answer when she heard a voice shouting at them.

“Move out of the way!”

the voice cried. Riya looked up just in time to see two girls crash into them.

They tumbled into a big heap.

"Ouch! Where did you

come from?" one of the girls asked.

"Are you new here in Sparta? I haven't seen you at Lake Demo before," the other asked.

"Where on Earth is–" Emma said, but Riya put her hand over Emma's mouth. Riya knew that they had to play along. They must not be

found out.

"Yes! We are new here," Riya nodded. "Please, tell us what we have missed!" The two girls stood up and helped Riya and Emma to their feet.

"My name is Leda," Leda said with a smile. "And this is Lyra."

"I'm Riya, and this is Emma," Riya said. She did her best to stay calm. Emma just stood there looking confused.

"Those are nice names!

Where are you from?" said Lyra.

"Um, far, far away," Riya replied. Emma stared at her.

"We were practising for the big race this afternoon." Leda said.

"Big race?" said Riya. Emma looked horrified and gulped.

"Yes! It's the Little

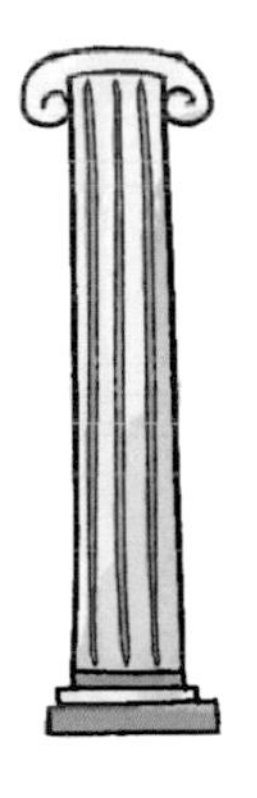

Olympics!" Lyra said. "It's a day when we do lots of sports! The big wheelbarrow race is the last event!"

"A sports day? Not again!" Emma groaned.

Chapter Three

Sunny Sparta

"So, you're telling me that magical gateways keep opening up around school and you have fallen in one before?" Emma said.

"Yes! I know it's hard to believe but look around you. We aren't in school anymore," Riya said.

"So, we have gone back in time and we are in Sparta

right now..." Emma said, thoughtfully. They could see a nearby town with tall columns everywhere and buildings with red tiles on the roofs. When Riya listened carefully, she could hear swords clashing and shields bashing as people trained. Emma turned to Riya. "Remember when Mr Meridell taught us

about Sparta and the Spartans in ancient Greece?"

"Of course, I don't ever forget Mr Meridell's lessons!" Riya said confidently.

"Mr Meridell said the Spartans were the toughest fighters. They were super scary, awfully angry and really, really strict!" worried Emma. "They made children do all kinds of fighting and training and cleaning up. And if the children didn't get all their work done in time, they were made to run one hundred laps around the field! Riya! What are they going to do to us? How do we get home?"

"There is something that we need to do," Riya said.

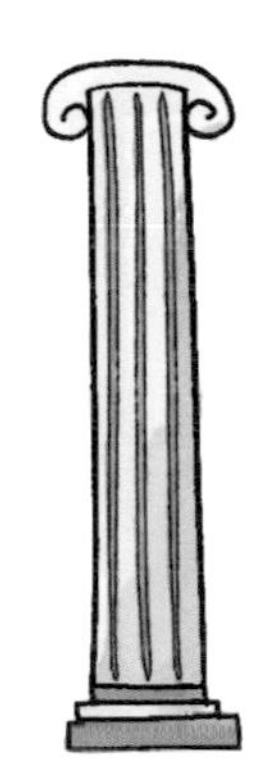

She tried her best to stay calm, but she did NOT want to fight or run or CLEAN. "There might be a problem we have to fix, or someone we need to help." Riya looked up at Lyra and Leda. Lyra was trying to get hold of Leda's feet so they could race, but they were struggling. They looked like they were rubbish at wheelbarrow racing! Were they really sporty, scary Spartans or were they just like Emma and Riya?

"It looks like they need our help," Riya realised.

"Wait! How do we know they won't attack us

or do something nasty?" Emma said.

"They won't! They didn't do anything horrible before. Come on, we have to try something, or we will be stuck in Sparta forever!" Riya said.

Riya and Emma walked over to Leda and Lyra slowly. Emma couldn't shake her fear and hid behind Riya.

Lyra waved brightly.

"W-we are going to help you!" Riya burst out.

"Excellent!" said Lyra. "We were hoping you would say that. You see, Leda and I want to win the wheelbarrow race. There are so many sporty girls in our class."

"But there's just one thing..." said Leda.

“We are really, really bad at wheelbarrow races!”

Chapter Four

Training Day

“Ready, set, GO!” Lyra and Leda set off, scrambling down the field. It went well for a couple of seconds before Leda’s arms suddenly gave way and they both fell to the ground.“Ouch!” Leda cried, as the dust settled around them. “I’m not strong enough!”

Emma thought hard.

“Well, it’s obvious isn’t it? You should swap over. Lyra go on the floor and Leda do the running,” Emma said.

“But… I don’t think I can

do it…" Lyra said. She looked a little shy.

"Why not? Are you not a super Spartan? Is this the Spartan way?" Emma said loudly. "Just try it and see what happens!" Lyra looked a little afraid of Emma, but she got down to the ground anyway. Lyra's arms wobbled a little bit, but she held herself up. Riya turned to Emma.

"You're so nasty!" Riya whispered to Emma. "She's trying her best!"

"If they win, it means we get to go home," Emma said. "I'm not messing around! I don't want to be here any longer."

"What if this doesn't

work and we are still stuck here?" Riya said, but Emma was watching Leda and Lyra. Lyra was a little better than Leda and they made it a little farther before they had to stop.

"They're rubbish!" Emma said. "Come on Riya, we can show them how it's done!" Riya didn't want to at first.

Emma wasn't her friend, they were rivals! But Emma was right, they had to work together to get home – and they had been good at wheelbarrow races in the past. Lyra and Leda came back over, and Emma got on the floor. Riya picked up Emma's feet. Riya started explaining it

to Lyra and Leda.

"Look at Emma's arms and legs. You can go faster if you do it like this," Riya said. "Ready Emma?"

"Ready!"

"And go!" The two of them dashed down the field. It was a little tough as the dust blew in their faces, but they went a lot farther than Leda and

Lyra had. Leda and Lyra started cheering.

"You two are amazing!" Lyra said.

"Are you competing in the wheelbarrow race?" Leda asked. "I just know that you'll win."

"No, we aren't," Riya said. What if a grown-up saw them? They would get in huge trouble. And even if they were good at wheelbarrow racing, they weren't friends anymore, so they couldn't race together!

Chapter Five

The First Race

Riya and Emma pushed Leda and Lyra all morning. They practiced races, push-ups and sprints to get ready. Leda and Lyra improved a little bit, and Riya was excited to see them race. Emma still thought that they had no chance of winning, but she

didn't say it out loud. Before they knew it, the time to race had arrived.

"There are two races," Leda explained. "So, we get two chances at winning."

"Are you sure you don't want to race?" Lyra asked. "You two make a really good team."

Emma watched as the

other racers lined up in their pairs. Each pair looked fierce, strong and ready to fight. Emma swallowed and put on a brave face for Leda and Lyra.

"We definitely cannot race! We are not a team! Anyway, best of luck to you both!" Emma said, as she patted Lyra's shoulder. "Riya and I will watch from over there... far, far away from any of those beasts," she added under her breath.

"Is that their teacher?" Riya whispered to Emma,

pointing to a terrifying looking woman. She was dressed in armour and had a sword at her hip.

"Why does she need a sword?" Emma gulped. Riya and Emma stood away from everybody and watched as Leda and Lyra lined up with the other racers. Riya bounced around on her tiptoes. She couldn't keep still.

"I hope they don't come last!" Riya said.

"Shh! It's starting," Emma said. The entire field went silent, and then, **BANG!** A massive drum was hit to signal the start of the race, and the girls were off! Riya and Emma wanted to cheer for Leda and Lyra, but most of the crowd were quiet. Riya held her breath and looked. Leda and Lyra were in last place! The other racers sped ahead. They looked like scuttling spiders hurrying along the floor. There was no way Leda and Lyra could keep up.

"Go! Go!" Riya started cheering and clapping as loud

she could, “Go Leda! Go Lyra!”

“What are you doing?” Emma grabbed her arm. “Stop! Nobody else is clapping!” Riya was about to answer when a large shadow loomed over them...

“And who are you?” It was the scary teacher! They had been caught and were in big, big trouble!

Chapter Six

Make Way for the Wheelbarrow!

Lyra skidded in front of Riya, her arms out wide. Her face was covered in sweat and she was gasping for breath.

"Teacher! This is Riya and Emma, they are new here!" Lyra said.

"Riya and Emma? I've never heard of them," the teacher said in a low voice. "Well? What are you waiting

for? Get ready for the next race."

"Actually... we aren't racing," Emma said in a tiny voice, her eyes fixed on the teacher's sword.

"Line up now! You will race! Are you not Spartan?" the teacher barked. Emma's legs were shaking and she couldn't move. Riya grabbed her arm.

“Emma, come on. We can do it, let’s just try it and see what happens,” Riya had a sudden feeling that this is what they were sent here to do. “Just like we practised, I’ll hold your feet.”

Emma nodded and they walked over to the starting line with Leda and Lyra.

The other Spartan racers looked them up and down. Oh dear.

"We can do it," Emma said under her breath as she got onto the floor. Everything went silent as the racers took their positions. Riya's heart thumped in her chest. She was ready. She took hold of Emma's legs and...

3... 2... 1... **BANG!** The race started.

Riya and Emma jumped forward. Riya saw Leda and Lyra fall behind, but she couldn't do anything about

them now. Riya closed her eyes and ran with all

her might. She huffed and she puffed, pushing Emma along. Dust flew in the air, she heard Emma cough, but Emma did not give up. Her arms clambered along at top speed. They fell through the finish line and came to a stop. They were gasping for breath.

"Riya, we did it! We didn't

come last!" Emma spluttered and coughed with a mouthful of dust. Riya looked up. She could see a few pairs, including Leda and Lyra, still racing. Riya jumped for joy. They didn't come first, but they still beat some of the Spartan racers.

"I can't believe we didn't come last!" Riya sang as she

held Emma's hands and the two of them cheered. Leda and Lyra made it across the line. They had come last again, but they didn't seem

to care.

"You did it! We watched you the whole time!" Lyra said.

"You're true Spartans!" Leda laughed. The happiness didn't last long as the teacher came over.

"Everybody, line up!" she yapped. "It's time for the award ceremony!"

Chapter Seven

Little Laurel Bangles

Riya and Emma watched in awe as the teacher gave the top three wheelbarrow racers laurel wreaths. The laurel wreaths were small leafy crowns that sat atop their heads. The teacher turned to the rest of the racers.

"You shall each be presented with a laurel bangle. This will show that you took part in the race, and remind you that you lost it terribly," the teacher growled. Emma snorted.

"That's not so bad, at least we aren't being punished," she whispered to Riya.

The teacher put a little laurel bangle on their

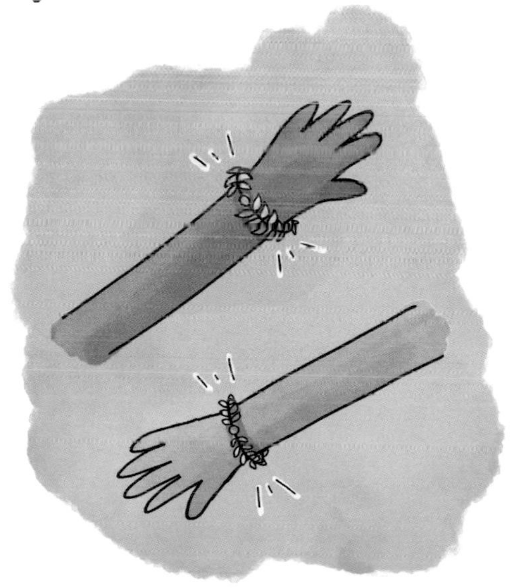

wrists and stepped back.

"And now..." the teacher said glaring at them, "... you will be punished. One hundred laps around this field, starting right now." Riya's face fell. Emma groaned loudly. "NOW!" the teacher shouted.

So, they ran. Leda and Lyra turned out to be much

better at cross country running and they jogged ahead happily, leaving Riya and Emma in last place. The Sun was hotter than before, the dust was in the air and there was nobody near them. Emma was too angry to think straight.

"This is EXACTLY where we started off at school,"

she moaned. “What was the point of the wheelbarrow race?”

“I don’t know, but it was kind of fun,” Riya admitted.

“Yeah... it was,” Emma agreed and just like that, the ground beneath their feet fell away. The world around them disappeared and they were falling through the gateway.

Colours flashed before their eyes. Emma reached out for Riya and held her close.

"Wooo!" Emma cheered and laughed. They landed on

soft, green grass. They were both in their PE kit again.

"No more scratchy dress!" Emma smiled.

"There you two are,

did you get lost?" it was Mr Meridell.

"Um... not exactly," Riya said. Emma bit her lip, so she didn't laugh.

"Well, you both came last I'm afraid. But it was a good effort," he smiled and then said with a wink, "don't worry, I won't make you run one hundred laps of the field."

Riya stood up and looked at Emma. Emma's eyes were wide open in shock. Riya reached out to help Emma up and the laurel bangle slid down her wrist.

"By the way, nice laurel bangles," Mr Meridell said as he walked away.

"Is he...? Does he...?" Emma stammered.

It seemed like Mr Meridell knew something about the gateways, but Riya would have to ask him another day. Sports day was over, and it was time to go home.

Meet the author:
Shalini Vallepur

Passionate about books from a very young age, Shalini Vallepur received the award of Norfolk County Scholar for her outstanding grades. Later on she read English at the University of Leicester, where she stayed to complete her Modern Literature MA. Whilst at university, Shalini volunteered as a Storyteller to help children learn to read, which gave her experience and expertise in the way children pick up and retain information. She used her knowledge and her background and implemented them in the books that she has written for BookLife Publishing. Shalini's writing easily takes us to different worlds, and the serenity and quality of her words are sure to captivate any child who picks up her books.

Meet the illustrator:
Amy Li

Born in Derby, Amy has always wanted to become a children's book illustrator, ever since falling in love with the work of Nick Sharratt and Quentin Blake as a child. She achieved a first class degree in Graphic Design and Illustration at De Montfort University before beginning her career at BookLife, during which time she has designed and illustrated over 100 titles. Amy's illustrations are always colourful, bright and full of life, and bound to draw in any child who picks up one of her books. Amy now resides in Norfolk, where she lives with her partner and cat.